C2

POLAR BEAR
BROTHERS

POLAR BEAR BROTHERS

by YLLA

Story by Crosby Newell

Designed by LUC BOUCHAGE

HARPER & ROW, PUBLISHERS, NEW YORK, EVANSTON, AND LONDON

POLAR BEAR
BROTHERS

Once there was a young polar bear.

He was bigger than a lollipop.

He was bigger than a little cat.

He was bigger than a big bass drum.

But he was not so large as his mother and father.

And he was smaller than his big brother.

He lived in a cold, crisp world.

He swam in a cool green pool.

And he wanted someone to play with him.

"Hey," he called to his big brother, "come and play with me.
Come and play with me in this cool green pool."

His big brother wasn't listening.
He was dreaming of snowmen and
snowflakes and frost.

The little brother pushed himself
away on a wave.
He floated through the green water.
"I don't care," he sang, "I don't care."
He looked at the sky.
He watched a small white cloud
floating all alone too.
He heard a bee buzz to another bee.
He was all alone
in his pool
in the sun.

"I don't care," he sang, "I don't care."

But he did care, and he floated in a lazy, lonely circle.

He counted his toes, and three sparrows in the sky.

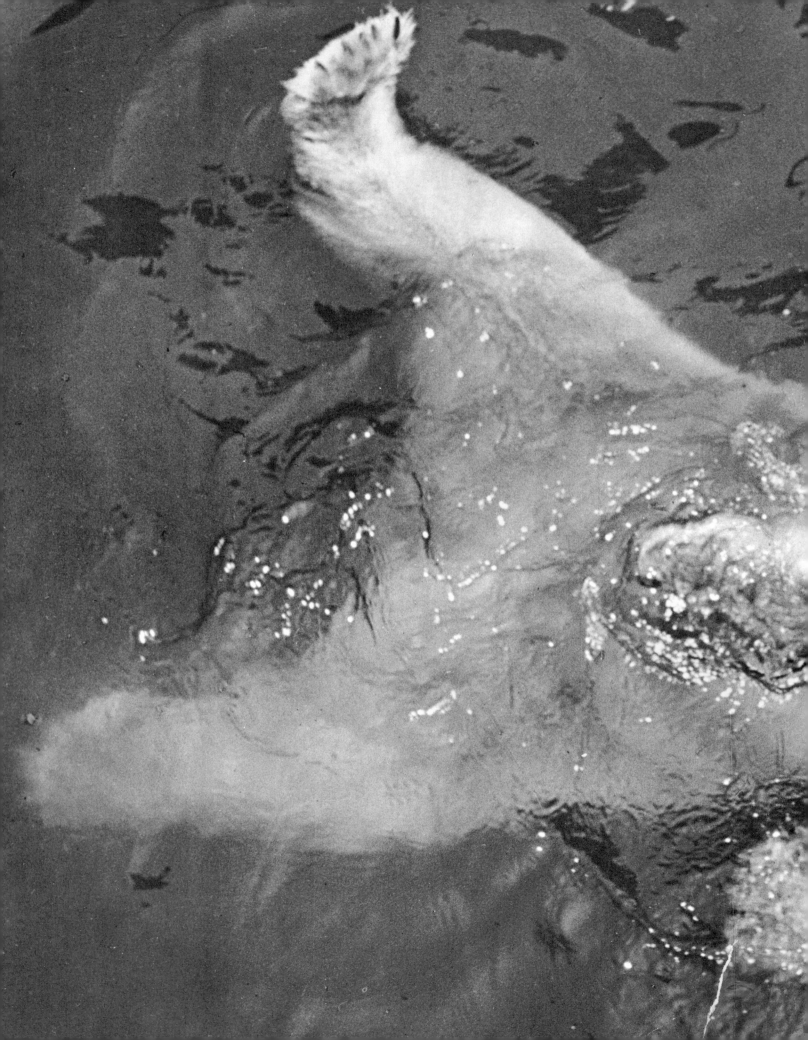

He stretched out so ——————— big
and hoped his mother was watching.

Someone else was watching.
His sleepy big brother lying in the sun
was watching.
"Move over there," said the big brother.
"Step aside," said the big brother.

"For I'm bigger than you are," said the big brother.

"And I need lots and lots of room for me."

And his big brother held his breath and flipped his feet

and landed head first— K E R · P L U N K

Now there were two young polar bears
in the cool green pool.

There were two polar bears and a round red barrel.

And what could two polar bears do with a round red barrel?

Could they hide in it?

Slide in it?

Ride in it?

No.

Could they fish in it?

Swish in it?

Wish in it?

No.

The best thing for a little brother to do with a round red barrel
was toss it across at a big brother waiting.

So he did. Then he swam very fast to catch up.

He was right there when his big brother caught the barrel
between his chin and his paws.
Could you do that?

"I could do that," cried the little brother.
But his big brother was watching
a ladybug who was watching him.

"I could do that, I think," cried the little brother.
"Not you," said his big brother, "you're too little,"
and he pushed him with a soft paw.

Around and around they rolled in the pool in the sun.
And they splashed and they tickled each other
and they laughed in that pool in the sun.

Then they were all—out—of—breath.

When the little brother couldn't think of one other game to play,

his big brother swam away from him toward
the shadows on the shore.

"So long," the big brother
called over his shoulder.
"Go play with the barrel.
Play with the barrel
all by yourself,
for I'm too busy
to play
any more."

And the big brother stretched out and
dreamed again of snowmen and snowflakes
and frost. And of a little brother
waiting to play. Tomorrow.

"I don't care," sang the little brother, pushing a paw
and tossing a toe in the air. "I don't care." But he wondered
all the same how long it would take tomorrow to come.